First Time

Going on an Airplane

Melinda Beth Radabaugh

Heinemann Library

Chicago, Illinois

© 2004 Heinemann Library
a division of Reed Elsevier Inc.
Chicago, Illinois

Customer Service 888-454-2279
Visit our website at www.heinemannlibrary.com

Designed by Sue Emerson, Heinemann Library; Page layout by Que-Net Media™
Printed and bound in the United States by Lake Book Manufacturing, Inc.
Photo research by Janet Lankford-Moran

08 07 06 05 04
10 9 8 7 6 5 4 3 2 1

Library of Congress Cataloging-in-Publication Data
Radabaugh, Melinda Beth.
  Going on an airplane/Melinda Beth Radabaugh.
       v. cm. – (First time)
Includes index.
Contents: What is an airplane? – Why do you go in an airplane? – What kind of airplane will you fly on? – What happens at the airport? – Who works on an airplane? – What happens when you get on the airplane? – How do you behave on an airplane? – What can you do on an airplane? – What happens when the airplane lands?
  ISBN 1-4034-3866-8 (HC), 1-4034-3881-1 (Pbk.)
  1. Air travel–Juvenile literature. 2. Aeronautics, Commercial–Passenger traffic–Juvenile literature. 3. Airports–Juvenile literature. [1. Airplanes. 2. Air travel.] I. Title. II. Series.
  HE9787.R33 2003
  387.7'42–dc21
                    5706   2002155329

Acknowledgments
The author and publishers are grateful to the following for permission to reproduce copyright material:
p. 4 George Hall/Corbis; p. 5 Debra Ashe/Index Stock Imagery; p. 6 Wil Blanche/Rex Intstock/Stock Connection/PictureQuest; p. 7 Jeff Greenberg/PhotoEdit Inc.; p. 8 Matt Bradley/Bruce Coleman, Inc.; p. 9 Image Bank/Getty Images; p. 10 SuperStock; p. 11 Ralf-Finn Hestoft/Corbis SABA; p. 12 Stone/Getty Images; p. 13 Greg Kiger/Index Stock Imagery; p. 14 David Brownell Photography; p. 15 Patrick Bennett/Corbis; pp. 16, 18, 19, 20 Robert Lifson/Heinemann Library; p. 17 Visuals Unlimited; p. 21 Francisco Cruz/SuperStock; p. 22 (row 1, L-R) Corbis, PhotoDisc; (row 2) PhotoDisc; (row 3, L-R) PhotoDisc, Corbis; p. 23 (row 1, L-R) Image Bank/Getty Images, SuperStock, Greg Kiger/Index Stock Imagery; (row 2, L-R) Stone/Getty Images, Stone/Getty Images, PhotoDisc; (row 3, L-R) Caron (NPP) Philippe/Corbis SYGMA, Robert Lifson/Heinemann Library, Corbis; (row 4, L-R) Robert Lifson/Heinemann Library, Ralf-Finn Hestoft/Corbis SABA, PhotoDisc; p. 24 (L-R) PhotoDisc, Corbis, PhotoDisc; Back Cover (L-R) Greg Kiger/Index Stock Imagery, Image Bank/Getty Images

Cover photograph by Creasource/Series/PictureQuest

Every effort has been made to contact copyright holders of any material reproduced in this book. Any omissions will be rectified in subsequent printings if notice is given to the publisher.

Special thanks to our advisory panel for their help in the preparation of this book:

Alice Bethke, Library Consultant
Palo Alto, CA

Eileen Day, Preschool Teacher
Chicago, IL

Kathleen Gilbert,
Second Grade Teacher
Round Rock, TX

Sandra Gilbert,
Library Media Specialist
Fiest Elementary School
Houston, TX

Jan Gobeille,
Kindergarten Teacher
Garfield Elementary
Oakland, CA

Angela Leeper,
Educational Consultant
Wake Forest, NC

Some words are shown in bold, **like this.**
You can find them in the picture glossary on page 23.

Contents

What Is an Airplane?

Airplanes are machines that fly in the sky.

People ride inside airplanes.

wings

engine

Airplanes have **engines** to help them fly.

They also have wings.

Why Do You Go on an Airplane?

Airplanes can take you far away.

Airplanes can go very fast.

Airplanes can take you on vacation.

They can take you to visit family.

What Kind of Airplane Will You Fly On?

You might fly in a small airplane.

It has narrow **aisles** and only a few seats.

aisle

You might fly in a big airplane.

It has many seats for many people.

What Happens at the Airport?

You show your **ticket** at the **check-in desk**.

You walk through a **security gate**.

You wait for your airplane.

Who Works on an Airplane?

Flight attendants help the **passengers.**

They also help the **pilot.**

Pilots fly the airplane.

They sit in the **cockpit**.

What Happens When You Get on the Airplane?

You meet the **flight attendants** and **pilots**.

You might get to see the **cockpit**.

Next, you find your seat.

The flight attendant helps with your **luggage**.

How Do You Behave on an Airplane?

First, you put on your **seatbelt**.

You listen to the **flight attendant's** directions.

You can play with toys or listen to music.

You talk in a quiet voice.

What Can You Do on an Airplane?

You may eat a **meal** or a snack.

You can bring books to read.

There may be a movie.

You can get up to go to
the bathroom.

What Happens When the Airplane Lands?

The **pilot** tells you to take off your **seatbelt**.

You get your **luggage**.

You get off the airplane.

You may find your family waiting to meet you!

Quiz

What can you find on an airplane?

Look for the answer on page 24.

Picture Glossary

aisle
pages 8, 9

flight attendant
pages 12, 14, 15, 16

pilot
pages 12, 13, 14, 20

check-in desk
page 10

luggage
pages 15, 20

seatbelt
pages 16, 20

cockpit
pages 13, 14

meal
page 18

security gate
page 11

engine
page 5

passenger
page 12

ticket
page 10

Note to Parents and Teachers

Reading for information is an important part of a child's literacy development. Learning begins with a question about something. Help children think of themselves as investigators and researchers by encouraging their questions about the world around them. Each chapter in this book begins with a question. Read the question together. Look at the pictures. Talk about what you think the answer might be. Then read the text to find out if your predictions were correct. Think of other questions you could ask about the topic, and discuss where you might find the answers. Assist children in using the picture glossary and the index to practice new vocabulary and research skills.

Index

Answer to quiz on page 22

You can find the luggage, the pilot, and the ticket on an airplane.

OCT   2005